About the Illustrator

Name: ....

Age: .... Hometown: ....

When I grow up, I'd like to be: ....

....

My favorite flying thing is: ....

If I could fly, the first thing I'd do would be:

....

I Can Fly?

COMPENDIUM®

kids™

inspiring possibilities.™

I still don't really know how
it happened, but today I
discovered I could fly. I was

reading at my school desk when my teacher called my name.

"Please sit down," she said. I wanted to say that I was already sitting when I realized I was

beginning to $float$ above my chair.
All the kids in my class looked
up at me and gasped.

"Maybe you should go down to the school nurse," my teacher said as I began to fly over her head.

She opened the door
and I drifted out, making
somersaults in the air all the
way down the hallway.

The nurse didn't know what was wrong. "I feel fine," I told her, but she said I should probably go home anyway. So I floated out the door and hovered over the playground.

I floated past the windows of my classroom and waved to my friends inside before I flew on.

Soon, the rooftops and treetops were so far below me that they looked like little toys. I couldn't even see people anymore.

Suddenly, everything looked white, and the air felt cool and wet.

I realized I was
flying through a cloud!

When I came up above the cloud, the sky was bright and clear and the clouds under my feet looked like soft white cotton puffs. They stretched as far as I could see.

Some of the clouds were tall like buildings, and others were flat like rivers and roads.

I wanted to explore the land of the clouds all day.

One by one, the stars appeared. The sun was setting, and the sky was turning orange and purple

and gold, and I realized
it was time to go home.
I drifted down to earth slowly.

My parents were waiting for me at home. "Where on earth have you been?" they asked with worry.

I smiled because I knew they'd never believe me.

WITH SPECIAL THANKS TO THE
ENTIRE COMPENDIUM FAMILY.

CREDITS:

Written by: M.H. Clark
Designed by: Julie Flahiff
Edited by: Amelia Riedler

ISBN: 978-1-935414-95-7

1st printing. Printed in China with soy inks. A0113030017500